D1234727

Going Shopping

SARAH GARLAND

Going Shopping

PUFFIN BOOKS

In you go.

Jump in, dog !

Down the road

and off to the shop.

Out of the car

and into the shop.

Shopping, shopping,

more and more shopping.

Pack it all up

and back to the car.

In you go

and home again.

PUFFIN BOOKS

Published by the Penguin Group
Penguin Books Ltd, 27 Wrights Lane, London W8 5TZ, England
Penguin Books USA Inc., 375 Hudson Street, New York, New York 10014, USA
Penguin Books Australia Ltd, Ringwood, Victoria, Australia
Penguin Books Canada Ltd, 10 Alcorn Avenue, Toronto, Ontario, Canada M4V 3B2
Penguin Books (NZ) Ltd, 182–190 Wairau Road, Auckland 10, New Zealand

Penguin Books Ltd, Registered Offices: Harmondsworth, Middlesex, England

First published by The Bodley Head 1982
Published in Picture Puffins 1985
Reissued in Puffin Books 1995
1 3 5 7 9 10 8 6 4 2

Made and printed in Italy by Printers srl – Trento